Darren Mackey was born in the Cathedral city of Armagh in 1973. He has lived with his wife Sharon and their three children, Conchur, Niamh and Caoimhin in the picturesque village of Benburb for the last twenty years. An avid music and football fan, he began his writing career at the ripe old age of forty and after considerable setbacks his first book *The Jolly Giraffe* was published in 2024. He is now currently working on the much anticipated follow up, a work entitled *The Glows*, which should be completed and published sometime in 2025.

i

DARREN MACKEY

THE JOLLY GIRAFFE

AUSTIN MACAULEY PUBLISHERS®
LONDON • CAMBRIDGE • NEW YORK • SHARJAH

A CIP catalogue record for this title is available from the British Library.

ISBN 9781035854950 (Paperback)
ISBN 9781035854967 (Hardback)
ISBN 9781035854974 (ePub e-book)

www.austinmacauley.com

First Published 2024
Austin Macauley Publishers Ltd®
1 Canada Square
Canary Wharf
London
E14 5AA

For Columbus.
I got your message, Dad.
I got your message.

Could I thank all the staff at Austin Macauley Publishers and my daughter, Niamh Mackey, for her proofreading and suggestions.

v

Chapter One

It had just past three, and in the jungle under the shade of the giant oak tree sat two of the forest's best friends. The first one was a monkey. His name was Mickey— Mickey the monkey, as he was known to his friends. And he was very, very grumpy. The second was a giraffe, a gentle giraffe called Jerry who was very, very jolly, and most of his friends in the jungle called him the jolly giraffe.

"I'm bored," grumbled Mickey the monkey.

"Bored?" said Jerry the giraffe.

"Yeah," replied Mickey the monkey. "Bored."

"Well then," said the jolly giraffe, jumping up onto his feet. "Do you want to dance?"

"Dance?" snapped Mickey the monkey. "I'm not sure if I know how to dance, Jerry."

"It's easy, monkey," replied the jolly giraffe. "All it requires is for you to move your feet and your body in different directions." For the next minute or so, Mickey the monkey glimpsed as he watched his friend jump around in the heat, doing a very enthusiastic rendition of the jungle jig. "What do you think, monkey?" he said before pirouetting into a moonwalk. "Do you want to join in?"

Mickey the monkey shook his head profusely. "No," he snapped. "I don't like dancing."

"You don't like dancing?" squealed the jolly giraffe. "But everybody likes dancing, monkey."

"Well, I don't," snapped the moaning monkey, folding his arms tightly across his chest. "Charlie the chameleon says that I have two left feet and can't dance."

The jolly giraffe sighed. "I'm sorry, monkey," he said. "I didn't know monkeys were born with two left feet. I guess that can be kind of difficult when you are buying new shoes." The moaning monkey sighed. "I don't have two left feet, Jerry," he said. "It's just a metaphor for not being able to dance."

"A whatafor?" said the jolly giraffe.

"A metaphor," repeated monkey, his smile thin. "It's a figure of speech. A polite way for someone to tell you that you can't dance."

"Poppycock," said the jolly giraffe. "There's no one in this entire forest who can say you can't dance, monkey. No one. And I mean no one. Especially not Charlie the chameleon. The last time I saw him dance was at Adam the Ant's wedding, and he danced no better or worse than anyone else."

The moaning monkey drummed his fingers on his arm. "Well, I don't," he said. "Now, can we please just drop it?"

The jolly giraffe took a deep breath. "Consider it dropped, monkey," he said, then sat back down beneath the shade of the big oak tree. "Consider it dropped."

From his purple backpack, the jolly giraffe pulled out a towel that was pink and fluffy and a bottle of cold water. After dabbing the moisture from his face and neck, he unscrewed the cap and tilted the bottle towards his lips. "Boy, it's hot," he said, pouring the refreshing liquid into his mouth.

"I suppose," said the moaning monkey, casting his eyes skyward.

"Oh, I'm sorry," said the jolly giraffe. "Would you like a drink?"

The moaning monkey shook his head. "I'm not thirsty," he said, resting his chin on his knee. "I'm bored, remember?"

"Yes, yes," said the jolly giraffe. "I remember." The moaning monkey watched as his friend drained the last of the water from the bottle. "Now," said the jolly giraffe after dabbing the side of his mouth with the towel, "what can we do to cheer you up?"

The two friends thought for a moment. And they thought. And thought. And just when they thought they could think no more. They thought. And thought. And thought some more. "I know," said the jolly giraffe, his green eyes wide, his long finger pointed skyward. "We could sing."

"Sing?" snapped the moaning monkey. "But I don't like singing, Jerry."

The jolly giraffe jumped up onto his feet. "Of course you like singing, monkey," he said, clapping his hands loudly together. "Everyone loves singing." The moaning monkey sighed, and even though he pressed the palms of his hands tightly against his ears, it still wasn't enough to drown out the jolly giraffe singing,

"In the forest, the mighty forest, the lion sleeps tonight."

Mickey the monkey gasped then jumped up onto his feet. "Shush!" he whispered, pressing the index finger of his right hand against his lips. "You don't want to wake Leo with all this talk of lions."

The jolly giraffe inhaled sharply. "Ohhh, I'm sorry," he said, looking nervously over his right shoulder and then his left. "I forgot about Leo. I really did. Do you want me to sing a little softer, monkey?"

Mickey the monkey frowned. "No," he said sharply. "I told you I don't like singing. Henry the hippopotamus said I sounded like a sick platypus."

"A sick platypus?" gasped the jolly giraffe. "I didn't know Penelope was unwell." The moaning monkey nodded his head. "Yeah," he said softly. "She has tons a…….. tonsa… you know, she has a sore throat."

"Tonsillitis," said the giraffe, his voice raised several octaves.

"Yeah," said monkey, "tonsil… tonsil…… she has a frog in her throat."

The jolly giraffe thought for a moment. What could he do to cheer up his dear old friend? Poor monkey didn't like dancing, and he didn't like singing, so what else was there left for them to do?

The idea made the jolly giraffe gasp. "I know," he said, his green eyes wide like frisbees. "Why don't we go and get something to eat?" For a moment, the moaning monkey sat in silence, pulling hard on his hairy chin.

"That's a good idea, Jerry," he said, licking his thick lips. "I haven't had a bite to eat since the banana buffet at breakfast."

The jolly giraffe jumped up and down for joy. "Oh, goody goody goody," he gasped, clapping his hands loudly together. "Oh, goody goody goody goody goody!"

"Calm down, Jerry," said monkey, holding up his hands. "All this jumping around is making me dizzy."

"Oh, I'm sorry, monkey," replied the jolly giraffe. "It's just that I am so excited. I have never been on a road trip before. Have you?"

The moaning monkey tutted loudly and cast his eyes skyward. "Of course, I've been on road trips before, Jerry," he said. "Why, just last week I attended Bouncing Betty's birthday bash in Burundi. And I went all by myself."

The jolly giraffe smiled. "You're so cosmopolitan, monkey," he voiced cheerfully. "So what are we waiting for, monkey? It's time for us to hit the road."

"Not so fast, Jerry," said monkey, holding up the index finger of his left hand. "We haven't discussed where we are going to go yet."

Chapter Two

With his hairy arms folded, the moaning monkey leant heavily against the trunk of the big oak tree. "I don't know how many times I have to say this, Jerry," he grumbled, "I don't like pizza."

The jolly giraffe sighed. "You don't like pizza, monkey?" he gasped. "But everybody likes pizza."

"Well, I don't," snapped monkey. "All the dough in the crust gives me…" he hesitated and cupped his hand over his mouth. "It gives me wind," he said softly.

The jolly giraffe sniggered.

"It's not funny, Jerry," snarled monkey. "It can be very uncomfortable, you know. Not to mention the embarrassment."

"I'm not laughing at you, monkey," protested the jolly giraffe. "Honestly, I'm not. The same thing happens to me when I eat beans."

"Beans," said the moaning monkey, his thick brows raised. "I heard beans can do that sometimes."

"Not sometimes," said the jolly giraffe. "All the time."

The moaning monkey nodded his head. "I'm sorry" he said "I can't go to Polly the Penguin's Pizza Palace with you. My insides just don't like bread."

The jolly giraffe smiled. "It's okay, monkey," he said, placing his hand on his friend's shoulder. "We all have the same body parts inside, so there's nothing for you to be embarrassed about. Everybody emits wind, monkey."

The moaning monkey sniggered. "They do?" he said.

"Of course," said the jolly giraffe, nodding his head gently.

"Even the king?" said monkey.

"Even the king," replied the jolly giraffe. "And the queen."

The moaning monkey gasped. "No," he said aghast. "Not the queen."

"Does she not have the same body part as you, monkey?" said the jolly giraffe.

The moaning monkey nodded. "I believe so," he said.

"And we all know her favourite food, don't we?" added the jolly giraffe.

"Brussels sprouts," hissed the moaning monkey.

"Precisely," said Jerry, nodding his head. "And we all know what happens to the body when your favourite food is Brussels sprouts."

"Wind," said monkey, his face awash with wonder. "You get wind." The jolly giraffe nodded his grand head and winked his right eye. "Exactly," he said. "So there's no need to feel embarrassed, monkey. Everyone who's anyone breaks wind."

"That's good to know, Jerry," said the moaning monkey. "It really is. But if it's okay with you, I'll pass on the pizza for now. Just to be on the safe side."

The jolly giraffe smiled. "That's okay, monkey," he said. "There's no point in going somewhere that makes you feel uncomfortable. Now, can we think of anywhere else?" For the next few moments, the two friends sat in silence, pondering plates of food they might want to indulge in.

"I know," said the jolly giraffe. "What about Jacko the Gecko's new granola bar?"

"Jacko the Gecko's new granola bar?" repeated monkey, his face awash with concern. "What's granola, Jerry?"

The jolly giraffe stuttered. "It's a... it's a..."

"It's a wha?" said Mickey.

"It's a new type of food that scientists say is good for your insides."

The moaning monkey nodded his head. "Sounds interesting," he said. "But what's in it?"

"Well," said Jerry, "there are oats."

"Oats," said Mickey. "I like oats."

"And there are raisins."

"Raisins," said monkey, licking his lips eagerly. "I like raisins."

"And there's honey."

The thought of runny honey drizzled all over his food made the moaning monkey purr like a contented cat. "I love honey," he said, his jaw slightly ajar. "It's my absolute favourite." "Well," said the jolly giraffe, "if you like that, you're going to love this." With his face beginning to burn red with excitement, the jolly giraffe paused for a moment just to make sure he had his friend's utmost attention.

"NUTS," he squealed loudly, his arms waving frantically in all directions. "They cover the whole thing in nuts, monkey!"

"NUTS!" screamed the moaning monkey, his long arm flailing wildly into the air. "DID YOU SAY NUTS, JERRY?"

The jolly giraffe hesitated. He wanted to say something positive. He wanted to say something soothing. He wanted to say anything that might help to calm his irate friend. Yet, no matter how hard he tried, the words he wanted to use failed to form and remained caught somewhere between his throat and teeth.

"DON'T YOU KNOW I'M ALLERGIC TO NUTS, JERRY?" screamed the moaning monkey, kicking wildly at the dirt that sat loosely on the baked ground. For a moment, the jolly giraffe stood motionless like a statue, his eyes wide and lips pushed into a small 'o'. "I'm sorry, monkey," he said after what felt like an eternity. "I didn't know you had a nut allergy."

"The worst kind," snapped Mickey. "Even the smell of nuts can send my body into shock." The jolly giraffe swallowed hard. "Again, monkey," he said gingerly, "I'm sorry. I didn't know how dangerous that could be for you or I would never have mentioned it."

The moaning monkey sighed and rubbed his flustered face with his hands. "It's okay, Jerry," he said. "It's partly my fault. With all this hanging around I do, I guess I didn't have time to tell you about it."

The jolly giraffe released a long, loud sigh of relief as he felt his shoulders begin to loosen. "Well, now that I know," he said, "you won't ever hear me mention the word…"

"Shush," said Mickey the monkey, pressing his finger against his lips. "Don't say it, Jerry. I never want to hear that word again. Okay?"

The jolly giraffe nodded his great head. "Understood," he said with both of his thumbs raised skyward. "Understood."

It took another bout of huffing and puffing before the two friends sat back down beneath the big oak tree. The smile that once decorated the jolly giraffe's face had now levelled out as the pressure to make his friend happy was beginning to show. He needed something special. Something spectacular. He needed something that was going to put a permanent smile back on the face of his old friend. He needed…

When he jumped up, the sudden movement startled the moaning monkey. "What is it, Jerry?" he said, suddenly snapped from his afternoon slumber.

"I don't know why I didn't think of it before, monkey," he said, his neck craned towards the sky.

"Think of what, Jerry?" offered monkey, his mind filled with expectations.

"Two words," said the jolly giraffe, his lips curling upwards into a smile, his chest pushed out triumphantly. "Ravenous Rhinos."

Chapter Three

The jolly giraffe didn't expect his friend to sit back down beneath the shade of the big oak tree. "Didn't you hear me, monkey?" he said. "I said Ravenous Rhinos."

"I heard what you said, Jerry," replied monkey, his arms folded tightly across his chest. "It's just that I er..." he hesitated.

"Just what?" said the jolly giraffe.

"It's just that Ravenous Rhinos are the whole way across the forest."

"Yeah, so?"

"Well, it will be dark by the time we get there."

"Yeah," said the jolly giraffe, "and your point is?"

The moaning monkey swallowed hard. "It's just that I don't like the jungle at night."

The jolly giraffe frowned. "You don't like the jungle at night, monkey?"

The monkey shook his head. "No," he said softly. "It's filled with all sorts of creatures that are hairy and scary."

The jolly giraffe laughed. "But monkey," he voiced, "what creature is more hairy and scary than you?"

"I'm not scary," snapped Mickey.

"I know you're not scary, monkey," said the jolly giraffe, "but someone who might not know you as well as I do might think you're scary."

The moaning monkey unfolded his arms and stood up. "Do you think so?" he said, leaning his back against the tree. "Do you think I look scary?"

"Not to me, you don't," offered the jolly giraffe. "But with those big long arms and sharp teeth, it's not hard to see why some strangers might think you're a little scary."

"But I'm more scared of them than they are of me," protested the moaning monkey.

The jolly giraffe nodded his head gently. "I know, monkey," he said, "I know you're more scared of them than they are of you. But sometimes looks can be deceiving. And in the middle of the jungle at night, you would look pretty scary yourself."

The moaning monkey snorted. "I suppose you're right, Jerry," he said. "If I did bump into someone as hairy and scary as myself, I would be pretty frightened, to tell you the truth."

"It is only natural to be scared of something, monkey. Most creatures are. But there's nothing to be scared of in the jungle. Especially at night. All the big, hairy, scary creatures have usually tucked in for the night, so we will have the jungle pretty much to ourselves."

Mickey the monkey inhaled deeply through his nose. "I suppose you're right," he said. "There's nothing out there to be afraid of, even at night. So do you think we could make it?"

"Do I?" squealed the jolly giraffe, bouncing up and down with delight. "There's nothing the jungle can throw at us that we can't handle, monkey. Especially if we stick together." Leaving the shade of the big oak tree, the two friends began to walk.

"Tell me, Jerry," said Mickey, "is the food in Ravenous Rhinos that good?"

"So good," replied the jolly giraffe, "that they wrote a song about it."

"A song?"

"Yeah," said the jolly giraffe. "Do you want to hear it?"

"Not reall......"

"When your feeling a little hungry
And you need to shake the blues
There's a place outside the jungle
Were the burgers are always huge
There's chips and french fried onions
There's steak and chocolate cake
And if you need a little extra
You can always refill your plate
So make no bones about it
Unless you love the ribs
The place is ravenous rhinos
Your home outside your crib"

When The Jolly Giraffe opened his eyes his friend began to clap. "Whooooooo" shouted Monkey "I didn't know you could sing Giraffe"

The Jolly Giraffe felt the blood rush to his face. He didn't like singing in public; indeed the only place he truly let go was in the shower on a Sunday morning. "I have been singing for a while now Monkey. Not professionally mind you but in my spare time

"You're really good," said Mickey, nodding his head. "Have you ever thought of entering Jungle got talent."

The Jolly Giraffe sniggered. "Don't be silly Monkey" he said bashfully. "I'm not good enough to sing in front of Simon the sloth"

"Oh I don't know Jerry " said Monkey "I watched the whole thing last year and your better than anyone I saw. Even the winner. What's his name"

"Bert"

"That's it" said Monkey, his hand shaped like a gun and pointing menacingly towards his friend. "Berty the beaver won it last year and he wasn't that overly special"

"Yes he was"

"No he wasn't" said Monkey, his weapon still cocked and loaded. "Tell you what. That other girl he beat in the final. What did you call her"

"Samantha"

"That's right" said Monkey. Samantha. Wasn't she a deer or something

The Jolly Giraffe smiled. "She was a sambar"

"A what bar"

"A sambar" said The Jolly Giraffe "it's a type of deer found in Southern Asia"

"Cool" said the Moaning Monkey "well she had a far better voice"

"Do you think so"

"Know so" replied Monkey, his weapon now lowered and resting by his side. "She should have won it"

Trying to ignore the fluttering in his stomach The Jolly Giraffe continued to walk. "Come on" he said looking back over his shoulder at his friend. "All this talk of singing competitions is going to leave us late"

"You're right," said Monkey, looking at his watch. "It has already past five and it will take us a good three to four hours to get there."

"If we're lucky" mumbled Jerry

"What" said Monkey

"Nothing" said The Jolly Giraffe with a smile. "Come on let's go"

In silence the two friends began to walk. One thinking about all the delicious food they were about to experience. The other dreaming of a contest. A contest he might enter one day. And perhaps. Just perhaps. Win.

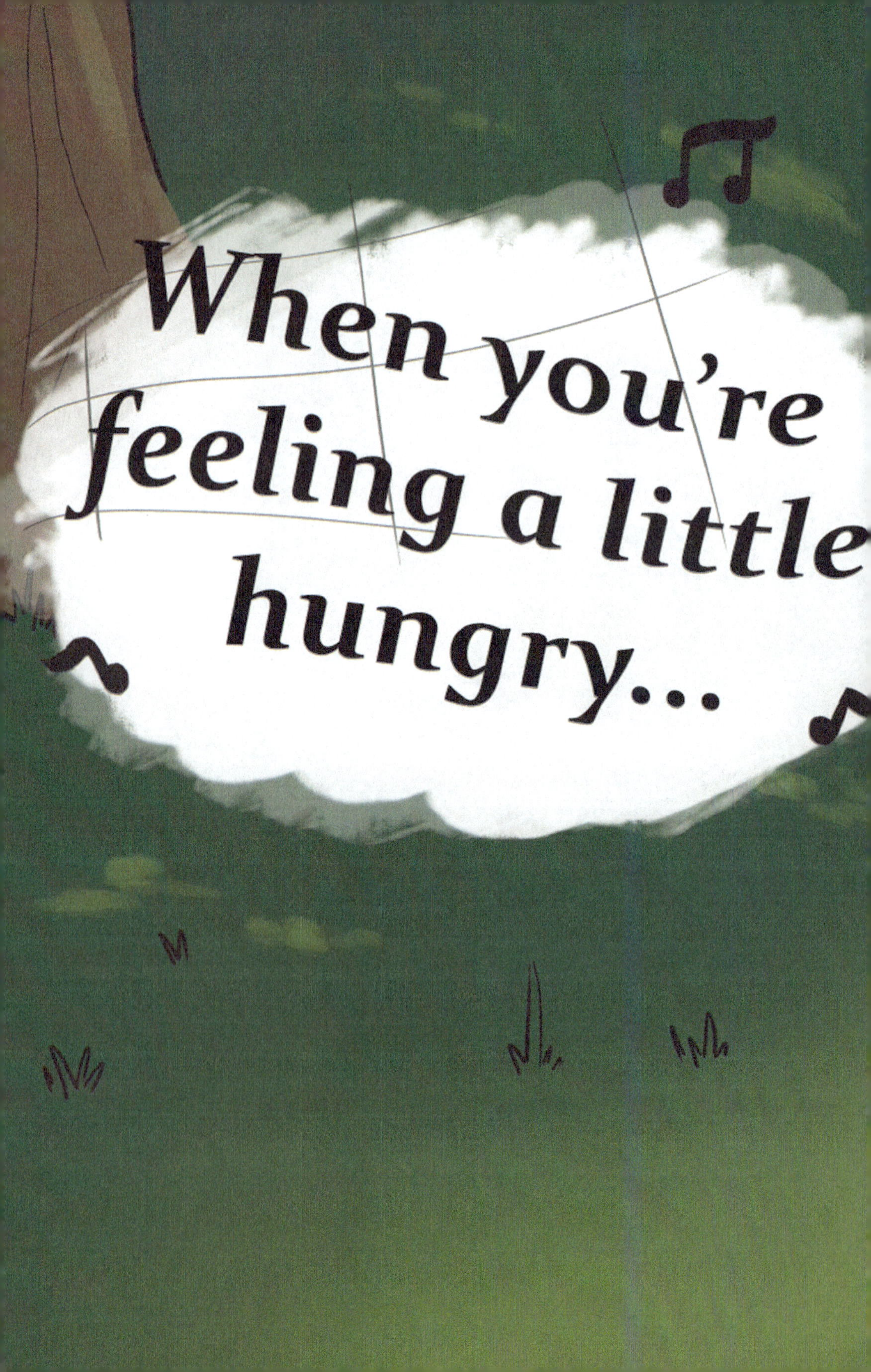
When you're feeling a little hungry...

Chapter Four

With the light slowly fading, it didn't take long before the forest resembled the inside of a cave. The trees, once bustling with the sound of song and vitality, had descended into an eerie silence, and the uneasy peace sent a shiver of fear rippling up the spines of the two trembling friends.

"Monkey" whispered the jolly giraffe "I didn't expect the jungle to be as dark and quiet as this"

The moaning monkey shook his head. "Me either," he said, gripping the arm of his friend tightly. "Do you think it's too late for us to turn back?"

"Not at all," replied the jolly giraffe. "The only thing I'm concerned about is the number of carrots I have eaten."

The moaning monkey looked at his friend. "Why do you say that, Jerry?" he pondered, his brows knitted.

The jolly giraffe bit down heavily on his bottom lip. "Well," he said, "if I had consumed more carrots, monkey, then perhaps I might be able to see in the dark."

The moaning monkey snorted. "Well," he said, his body quivering like a bowl of jelly on a malfunctioning roller coaster, "If it's any consolation, my friend, I grew up on a diet of carrots and bananas, and I can't see my finger in front of my face."

"Sweet," said the jolly giraffe. "So the carrot thing is all just a big lie?"

"Not at all," said Mickey. "Carrots are very good for you. Just like broccoli and cauliflower. But I'm afraid the old wife's tale about them helping you see in the dark is a little far-fetched, to say the least."

Suddenly, the silence was splintered by a sharp rustling noise that came from behind.

"Monkey" wheezed the jolly giraffe.

"Yes?" replied Mickey.

"Can you please let go of my neck? You're strangling me."

The moaning monkey gasped. "Oh, I'm sorry, Jerry," he said, retracting his claws ever so slightly. "But I think there's something in those bushes."

The jolly giraffe coughed twice. "Do you think it's something big, monkey?" he said softly.

The moaning monkey nodded. "Absolutely," he whispered. "And I have no doubt it's something scary."

"Not scary as well," said the jolly giraffe. "You know I don't like scary things."

"Me neither," added monkey. "But there's no doubt whatever is hiding in those bushes is hairy, scary, and very, very hungry."

The jolly giraffe gulped. "Hungry," he said. "Why do

you think it's hungry, monkey?"

"Everything that lives in the jungle is hungry, Jerry."

"You never mentioned that before, monkey."

"I'm sorry, Jerry," said monkey. "It only popped into my head now."

"And what is it you think it eats?" whispered the jolly giraffe.

The moaning monkey paused for a moment. "Chargrilled giraffe, I hope."

"That's not funny, monkey," spat the jolly giraffe.

"It wasn't supposed to be funny, Jerry," said monkey, his teeth chattering loudly. "But in this volatile situation, I'm afraid it's every primate for themselves."

With their breath held and eyes peeled more than four bananas, the two friends watched as the branches parted and out onto the path popped Leo. Leo the lion. Leo yawned. "What's all the fuss about?" he said, scratching his behind.

The two friends tried. They tried to scream. They tried to run. Yet no matter how hard they tried, they could neither scream nor run.

"Do you see that, Jerry?" said monkey.

"I do," replied the jolly giraffe.

"Did I not say the jungle was dark?"

The jolly giraffe nodded his head. "You did, monkey. Indeed you did."

"And did I not say the jungle was scary?"

"I'm afraid you did, monkey. You said the jungle was scary."

The moaning monkey swallowed hard. "And did I not say that some big, hairy, and scary creature was going to eat us up?"

"You did, monkey. Those were your exact words."

"And Jerry. Can you please tell me. Have you ever seen a more hairy and scary beast than the one who has just popped out from those bushes?"

The jolly giraffe shook his head. "No, monkey," he said, "I have never seen a hairier or scarier beast than the one who is standing in front of us right now." The moaning monkey groaned. "I hate it when I'm right, you know. Hate it."

"So do I, monkey," said the jolly giraffe. "What do you think we should do now?"

"There's only one thing for us to do now, Jerry."

"What's that, monkey?"

"RUN!"

With his eyes closed and arms flapping in all directions, the jolly giraffe began to run. He ran round and round, screaming at the top of his voice for someone to come and help. It wasn't until he felt dizzy—really light-headed—that he stopped. With the world still spinning when he opened his eyes, the jolly giraffe fell to the ground. "What are you doing?" screamed monkey. "That beast is going to eat you!"

"No, I'm not," said Leo the lion.

"Don't listen to him, Jerry," pressed monkey from somewhere high above. "He's going to have you for supper."

Leo the lion yawned. "No, I'm not," he insisted. "I'm a vegetarian."

"A veg-what-ian?" asked the jolly giraffe.

"A vegetarian," repeated Leo. "I only indulge in plants and fruit."

"He's lying!" screamed monkey. "Who ever heard of a lion who only eats plants and..." he paused. "What was the other thing he said?"

"Fruit," said Leo and the jolly giraffe at the same time.

"Prove it!" shouted monkey, his hand cupped over his mouth.

Leo the lion tutted. "This is ridiculous," he muttered under his breath. "Nobody ever believes me when I say I'm vegetarian. Nobody." From the pocket of his chequered waistcoat, Leo the lion pulled a piece of laminated plastic and handed it to the jolly giraffe.

"What is it?" said monkey.

"It's some kind of badge," said the jolly giraffe after a brief inspection.

The moaning monkey tutted. "I know it's a badge, Jerry," he grumbled. "But what does it say?"

The jolly giraffe cleared his throat. "'To whom it may concern,' he read slowly and carefully so as not to make any mistakes. 'This badge is doc...doc...doc...'"

"Documented," said Leo with a nod.

"Thank you," said Jerry. "Documented confirmation that Leo the lion..."

"That's me," said Leo with a smile.

"That's him," said Jerry, pointing his finger at Leo.

The moaning monkey sighed. "I know who he is, Jerry," he said. "Now will you please hurry up?"

"Sorry," said the jolly giraffe. "Now, where was I?"

"Leo the lion," snapped monkey.

"That's me," said Leo.

"That's him," said the jolly giraffe.

From the trees, the moaning monkey swooped down and snatched the piece of plastic from the jolly giraffe's hand.

"Hey!" said the jolly giraffe. "I was reading that."

"You're too slow," snapped Mickey the monkey, raising the badge towards his face. "I could have had a novel finished by now."

The jolly giraffe puffed out his cheeks. "The cheek of some people," he mumbled under his breath. "The absolute cheek." They watched in silence as Mickey the monkey scanned the card.

"Well?" said the jolly giraffe. "What does it say?"

Mickey the monkey tutted loudly before handing back the badge. "It says that by all accounts, our friend here is indeed a fully-fledged vegetable."

"Vegetarian," corrected Leo, his voice raised several octaves. "And I can proudly say I have been since birth."

The jolly giraffe blew out his cheeks. "That's brilliant," he said, clapping his hands loudly. "Just brilliant."

"Well," said the moaning monkey. "Now that we have that little issue cleared up, we shall be on our way. Come on, Jerry, let's go."

Leo the lion shuffled uneasily on his feet. "May I be so intrusive as to inquire as to the whereabouts of your excursion?"

"To what now?" said the jolly giraffe.

Leo the lion smiled. "Where are you off to, my good fellow?" he said, tilting his cap.

"Nowhere," spat the moaning monkey. "We are just out here looking for a new..." he hesitated. "...a new tree, that's it. We are on the lookout for a new tree."

"In the dark?" said Leo the lion.

"No better time," said Mickey, scratching at a phantom itch that he pretended was behind his ear. "You get a better feel for a place at night."

Leo the lion pulled hard on his chin. "I see," he said, his black eyes narrowing with suspicion. "And what about you, giraffe? Where are you going?"

"Ravenous Rhinos," said the jolly giraffe with a thick

smile. "We are going to Ravenous Rhinos," he began to sing. "We are going to Ravenous Rhinos. Ravenous, Ravenous Rhinos..."

The moaning monkey sighed and dropped his head into his hands. "Why do I even bother?" he mumbled to his pink palms. "Why? Why? Why? Why? Why?"

"So," said Leo the lion after letting the jolly giraffe finish his rendition, "which one is it?" The two friends glanced sideways at each other. It was monkey who winked first, followed by a nod of his head, then another wink, and one last nod of reassurance to indicate they were both on the same page. The two friends turned and smiled.

"Ravenous Rhinos," spat the jolly giraffe just as monkey was about to speak.

"No, Jerry," snapped Mickey the monkey.

"No?" gasped the jolly giraffe.

"I mean yes," said the moaning monkey, nodding his head. "I mean no," said the moaning monkey, shaking his head. "I mean we're... were... oh, never mind," he said, folding his arms. "We're going to Ravenous Rhinos for heaven's sake."

"Hooray!" shouted the jolly giraffe, turning toward Leo the lion. "Didn't I tell you, Leo, we were going to Ravenous Rhinos? Didn't I tell you?"

Leo the lion nodded his head. "You did, giraffe," he said, moving a step closer. "Now for my next question. Can I come?"

"No," snapped the moaning monkey.

"Yes," cried the jolly giraffe. "Of course, you can come with us, Leo. Isn't that right, Mickey?" he continued while jumping up and down. "Leo can come with us. Can't he, Michael? Leo can come with us to Ravenous Rhinos."

The moaning monkey breathed deep and turned. "What was the point," he thought? His best friend had just made friends with a lion. A hungry lion. A lion who hadn't eaten properly since birth. And now they were taking him to the biggest restaurant in the jungle. "Now we're having a laugh," shouted the Jolly giraffe as Mickey the monkey grimaced and hoped to himself that everything was going to work out okay.

Chapter Five

For what felt like an eternity, the party of three walked. Then they walked. And they walked some more. And just when they thought they could walk no more, they walked. "How much further?" whinged the moaning monkey. "We have been walking like forever, and my poor feet are killing me." Leo the lion stretched, yawned, then proceeded to scratch an itch that attacked the pits of his arms. "I know," he said, then yawned a second time. "It feels like I have been hiking for so long now that I have missed my morning nap, my afternoon siesta, two power naps, and four of my much-needed forty winks."

"Blimey," said the jolly giraffe, "you do like sleeping, Leo."

Leo the lion nodded his head. "Not really," he said. "I only sleep twenty-two hours out of the day. My brother Lucas, he's the lucky one. He gets to nap for twenty-three hours a day." The jolly giraffe flapped his lips like a horse. "Whooo," he said. "That's a lot of sleeping, Leo."

"It's the perks of being the king, I suppose," said Leo the lion. "There's sleeping and eating. Eating and sleeping. And then, when you think there can be no more sleeping or eating, there's another bout of sleeping."

"Enough talk about sleeping," snapped monkey, his hands balled into fists. "I want to know how long we have been walking for."

"Ok," said the jolly giraffe, "keep your hair on, monkey."

From the pocket of his ripped Levi jeans, the jolly giraffe pulled a thick chain. At the end of the gold chain swung a polished gold fob that was engraved with the letters JG. The jolly giraffe smiled at the full hunter before pressing down on the crown and opening the face. "Let me see," he said, blowing a little dust from the bezel. "We left the big tree at six. Is that correct?"

"Correct," confirmed monkey with a stern nod.

"And we met Leo."

"That's me," said Leo, pointing at himself.

The jolly giraffe laughed. "That's him," he said, pointing at Leo. "We met Leo at seven." "Yes. Yes," hissed the moaning monkey. "We know all that, giraffe. The only thing we don't know is the amount of time we have been walking."

"Well," said the jolly giraffe, ignoring the rude interruption, "if we found Leo."

"Don't say it," snapped monkey. "We all know who you are."

"At seven," continued the jolly giraffe, "and the big hand is pointing at twelve and the small hand is still pointing at seven, that means..."

"TWELVE HOURS!" squealed the moaning monkey, his eyes rolling back in his head. "We have been walking around this jungle for twelve hours."

The jolly giraffe paused. "I don't think so," he stuttered before checking the watch again to make sure of no discrepancies.

"Face it, Jerry," spat the moaning monkey. "We're lost. No one tramps around a jungle for half a day and pretends to know where they are going." He paused and put his hand on his hip. "And do you know who's going to find us?"

"The jungle patrol?," said the jolly giraffe.

"No! Not the jungle patrol!," spat the moaning monkey. "Those bunch of idiots couldn't find the jungle, never mind someone in it." The moaning monkey inhaled deeply. "No," he continued, "we are going to be found in roughly a hundred years from now by some intrepid explorer who just happens to stumble across our decomposed bodies while out looking for some long-forgotten city."

The jolly giraffe smiled. "Oh, silly monkey," he said, "we haven't been gone for twelve hours. We have been walking for twelve minutes, and in another ten to twelve minutes, we will be at the restaurant."

The moaning monkey's brows knitted. "You what?" he said sheepishly.

"We have only been walking for twelve minutes, monkey," confirmed the jolly giraffe, "and once I find out exactly where we are…"

"Hold up," interrupted monkey. "You don't know where we are?"

The jolly giraffe squirmed. "Of course, I know where we are, monkey," he said. "We are in the jungle. But I just need to figure out exactly where we are in the jungle so we can take the correct path to Ravenous Rhinos."

The moaning monkey frowned. "And how are you going to do that then?"

"You're going to climb a tree," said the jolly giraffe with a smile.

"Indeed I'm not," snapped Mickey, taking a small step back. "You know as well as I do that I'm afraid of heights. That's why I live on the ground."

"Interesting," said Leo the lion. "A monkey who is afraid of heights. Why, I have never encountered such a specimen before."

"Shut it, meat dodger," spat monkey. "Nobody asked you for your opinion. Just because I'm a monkey doesn't automatically mean that I am good with heights. Some of my friends have an allergy to banana juice, and no one freaks out about that. But say you don't like heights, and BOOM—suddenly everyone thinks you're a freak." Leo the lion held up his hands in surrender. "I'm sorry, monkey," he said. "I didn't mean to offend you, and I apologise for jumping to the conclusion that all monkeys should be able to climb trees. That was wrong of me, and I sincerely apologise."

The moaning monkey rubbed his nose with the back of his hand and breathed hard. "Why, just the other day, someone called me an imposter," he said, his gaze fixed firmly on the ground. "And the day before that, someone called me a ground hugger."

"A ground hugger," said the jolly giraffe. "Now, that's just rude."

"Don't you dare listen to them, monkey," said Leo the lion. "We love you just the way you are. And if you never want to climb a tree, we support you fully in that decision." From the corner of his lips, a smile curled up on Mickey the monkey's face. "Thank you, Leo," he said, offering out his hand. The jolly giraffe smiled as the two new friends locked hands. "Do you know, monkey," he said, "it's possible to conquer your fear one small step at a time." The moaning monkey sighed. "I don't know, Jerry," he said. "I have tried everything from hypnosis to herbal remedies, and nothing seems to have found the trick."

"Ahhhh," said the jolly giraffe, pointing his finger skyward. "But have you tried small steps?"

The moaning monkey frowned. "What do you mean by 'small steps'?" he said.

"Well," said the jolly giraffe, "as you might or might not know, I used to have a fear of spiders."

"Yes," said Mickey. "I remember that. And how did you overcome your phobia?" The jolly giraffe pressed himself closer. "Do you know Columbus the camel?" he said, his hand cupped over his mouth.

The moaning monkey nodded his head but remained silent.

"Well," continued the jolly giraffe, "Columbus the camel introduced me to Summer the spider, and each day for about a year, Summer came round to visit me. At first, all she did was talk in through the window. Then, as the months passed, she began to gradually come into the house, and it wasn't long before we were having fully-fledged conversations. Now, nearly a year later, I only scream for the first twenty minutes of our session, and she keeps reassuring me that it won't be long before I actually open my eyes."

Leo the lion began to clap. "Bravo, old chap," he said. "That's one way of conquering your fear. Small steps."

"Exactly," said the jolly giraffe. "Just take it one small step at a time. So if you're willing to try it, monkey, we can help you climb as far as you are willing to go."

Mickey the monkey breathed deep and pushed out his chest. "Ok, Jerry," he said, pushing his sleeves up towards his elbow. "If you think I can do it, then let's try and do it." The jolly giraffe punched the air with delight. "You go, monkey!" he shouted, then began to clap loudly.

Mickey the monkey walked over to the tree, then craned his neck.

"Don't look up," shouted Leo the lion. "Look ahead. The only thing you have to worry about is the first step."

The jolly giraffe smiled before placing his hand on Leo the lion's shoulder and squeezing. "Right, right," said the moaning monkey with a nod of his head. "The only thing I have to worry about is the first step," he mumbled beneath his breath. Ignoring the fluttering in his stomach, Mickey the monkey lifted his right foot from the ground and placed it gently upon the first branch of the tree. He paused for a moment, letting the oxygen flow in through his nose, hoping his expanding lungs could pacify the butterflies that were beginning to hatch in his tummy. When his left leg left the ground, he thought he heard a cheer, but his mind was filled with wonder and a nagging thought that perhaps butterflies emerge from cocoons rather than eggs. Up and up he climbed, never looking up or down, but always concentrating on what was in front. The higher he got, the more giddy he felt. He could feel his body become light—so light he could almost let go of the bark and just float away into the night sky like a big hairy balloon. "I should have done this years ago," he shouted, safe in the knowledge that he had climbed too far for the other two to hear.

"There's no need to shout," said the jolly giraffe. "We can still hear you, monkey." When Mickey the monkey opened his eyes, he couldn't believe it. "One step," he shouted, dropping down from the branch. "I have only taken one step!"

"That's all you need to take, monkey," said Leo the lion. "Remember, it's called small steps, and you mustn't forget that that small step was your first."

The moaning monkey sighed. "But I thought I was closer to the top."

"You were closer to the top," insisted the jolly giraffe. "You were closer to the top than you were this time yesterday," he added. "And if you like, we can come back tomorrow to see if you can conquer two, or perhaps three branches."

Mickey the monkey puffed out his cheeks and nodded his head. "I would like that," he said, craning his neck and trying to envisage the top. "You know," he added, with a smile, "one small step for primates, one giant leap for mankind." After looking at each other, the three friends burst out laughing.

"Now we're having a laugh," said the jolly giraffe. "Now we're having a laugh."

Chapter Six

It was only after the laughter had subsided that the three friends realised their predicament hadn't improved. "What are we going to do, Jerry?" asked the moaning monkey. "I do believe we are still lost."

"We're not lost," replied the jolly giraffe, "we're just a little..." he paused for a moment, scanning his grey matter for the correct terminology, "off course," he added with a smile. "We're just a little off course."

"Well," snapped the moaning monkey, "we need to get back on course soon because it won't be long before the light totally fades, Jerry. And I don't like the dark." Leo the lion yawned. "Me neither," he said, scratching the top of his head. "I'm normally sleeping at this time, so I don't get to see the really hairy and scary things that come out at night."

"That's it!" shouted the jolly giraffe as he began to rummage through his pockets. "Leo, you're a genius."

The two friends watched in silence as the jolly giraffe began to pull every item you could think of from his pocket. There was a camera, a pair of glasses, a spanner, an old coffee cup (with coffee still in it), a piano tuner, a can of tuna, a Rubik's Cube, a set of dice, a bicycle pump, a mobile phone charger, a broken kettle, a pair of earrings (he hoped belonged to his sister), a fake moustache, a can of soup, a potted plant, two decks of cards, a set of wipers he couldn't recall purchasing, a cuddly toy that had lost one of its eyes, a pancake maker, a set of crystal salt and pepper shakers, a bar of soap, a pair of striped pyjamas, nail clippers, a baseball cap, a football boot, another football boot, and another, a poster of his favourite football team Junglechester United, socks, the Racing Post, a pair of orange Speedos, swimming goggles, a fishing rod, the fourth football boot, and just when they had all given up hope, he pulled a long black pole that resembled a police baton.

"What is it?" inquired Leo the lion.

The jolly giraffe smiled. "It's a torch, Leo," he said, fumbling along the shaft for the switch.

"And what good's a torch?" said the moaning monkey.

The jolly giraffe sighed. "Oh, monkey," he said, "do you not remember Tiger Tim?"

"The actor?" said the moaning monkey, his lip curling upwards.

The jolly giraffe nodded his head. "Among other things," he said. "Most people don't realise just how much of a musician Timothy was. He could play the piano, guitar, saxophone…"

"Yeah, yeah, yeah," interrupted the monkey, "we all remember how fabulous old Timothy was. But what has he got to do with our current predicament, Jerry?"

The jolly giraffe tutted and raised an eyebrow. "Don't you remember the catchy theme they released when Ravenous Rhinos first opened?" he said. "You know, the one featuring Tiger Tim."

The moaning monkey drummed his fingers on the side of his face. "Catchy tune. Tiger Tim," he said. "Is that the one where they did that silly dance?"

"That dance wasn't silly, monkey," said the jolly giraffe. "That dance was a well-choreographed piece of art that started a dance craze around the world."

The moaning monkey shrugged his shoulders. "Just because it started some stupid dance doesn't mean it was any good, Jerry. Just look at Gangnam Style."

The jolly giraffe laughed. "Fair point," he said, grinning profusely to himself, "but this was catchy. Do you want me to sing it?"

"Not at all," said the monkey, "I would rather have my teeth pulled by an unqualified dentist with rusty tools and a lazy eye."

Ignoring the insult, the jolly giraffe cleared his throat and began to sing aloud.

There's no need to panic
When the Forest grows dark
There's no need to cry out
If you're missing that spark
So if you can't walk
Or if you can't fly
And
If you can't find your way, just look for the.......

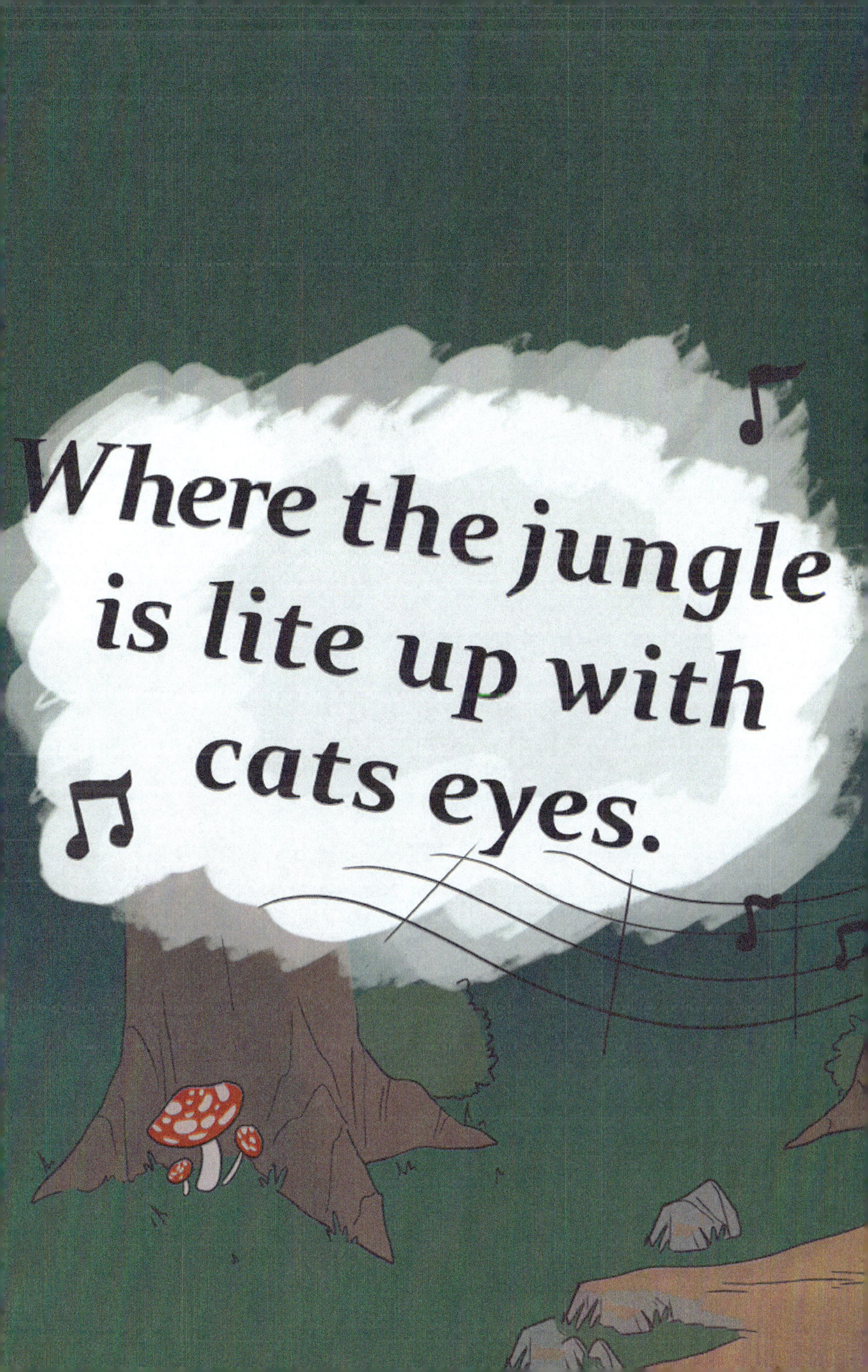

Where the jungle is lite up with cats eyes.

"Cat's eyes!" screamed the moaning monkey. "Jerry, you're a genius!" he said, kissing the jolly giraffe on the cheek.

The jolly giraffe blushed and batted his long eyelashes. "Thank you, monkey," he said, swinging his long legs at the grass.

"No, seriously, man," said Mickey the monkey. "You're a genius, Jerry. Now don't just stand there. Turn it on." It only took another moment of fumbling before the jolly giraffe located the elusive switch. "There you are," he said to no one in particular, and with a flick of a switch, he banished the dark and turned night into day.

"Man, that's bright," said Leo the lion, grimacing at the harsh light. "I didn't think it would be so bright."

The moaning monkey blinked. He couldn't help the tears that pooled in the corner of his eyes. "Don't point it at me, Jerry," he spat, covering his face with his arm. "Point it at the ground."

"Oh, I'm sorry," said the jolly giraffe, instantly dropping the beam to the floor. "I didn't realise I was blinding you."

The moaning monkey blinked, then dabbed the tears that had pooled in the corner of his eyes with the back of his hand. It took a moment, a moment of pinching the bridge of his nose with his thumb and forefinger before the harsh white spots began to melt. "Can anyone else see those lights on the ground?" he said, still blinking and squinting.

"For sure," squealed the jolly giraffe. "They are the cat's eyes Tiger Tim was singing so elegantly about."

It wasn't until another bout of blinking was completed that the jungle came back into complete focus. "Whoooo," said Mickey the monkey. "You could almost land a plane here; there's that many lights."

"I know," said the jolly giraffe. "Come on, let's go."

Like a pack of hungry bloodhounds, the three friends followed the glittering trail. They followed it over a hill, down a mountain, through a cave, across a stream, under a bridge, over a bridge, past a village, through a swamp, and just when it was on the tip of Mickey the monkey's tongue to ask how much further, out of the jungle they popped. Last to leave the thick foliage was the jolly giraffe. "Why have we stopped?" he said, still scanning the ground for light. "And why, monkey, does it look like you have seen a ghost?" Mickey the monkey did not speak. With his jaw ajar, he just raised his long arm and pointed. "What?" said Jerry, his eyes following the sea of hair that swayed gently in the summer breeze.

"What is it, monkey?" When his eyes jumped off the end of his good friend's darkened fingernail and came to rest on the large stone building that was moulded like a rhinoceros horn, the jolly giraffe gasped. "It's..." he stuttered, his eyes wide like vinyl, "it's..."

"It's magnificent," said Leo the lion, not noticing the jolly giraffe's thick nod of approval. "It sure is," offered Mickey the monkey, his arm still raised. "I mean, I heard it was big. But boy, this is way beyond any of my expectations."

"And that smell," said Leo the lion, sniffing the warm air. "What is that smell?"

The jolly giraffe took a step forward. "That's the scent of heaven, my friend," he said. "That's the scent of heaven."

Chapter Seven

No one could say who was the first to run. The moaning monkey said it was Jerry who took off first, while Leo the lion was of the notion that it was monkey who was first to break rank. Yet whoever it was, the three friends bombed up toward the door of Ravenous Rhinos like a pack of hungry cheetahs on petrol-propelled roller skates. Even though he had the longest legs, it was the jolly giraffe who reached the door last. "What kept you, Jerry?" teased the moaning monkey, his arm stretched out and leaning heavily against the glass. "We have been here for an hour."

The jolly giraffe wanted to smile. He wanted to tell monkey Frank Oliver. But the only thing he could do was draw deep the air that was filled with the sweet aroma of freshly baked doughnuts.

"Gosh, I'm so hungry," said Leo the lion, feeling his belly rumble for the first time. "I could eat the spot off a giraffe."

The jolly giraffe swallowed hard. "Now steady on, Leo," he said, his brows knitted, "there's plenty of food to go around. Besides, my spots look perfectly fine right where they are, thank you." Leo the lion blushed. "I'm sorry, Jerry," he said, rubbing his tummy, "it's just a metaphor we use when we're really hungry. It predates a time when we lions had to go out and forage for ourselves. Now, we are much more civilised, Jerry, with Jungle Eats and Deliverroots. The jolly giraffe nodded his grave head. "Well, that's okay," he said nervously, "let's just keep it like that and leave my spots just where they are."

Leo the lion held up his hands. "I'm sorry," he said, "I guess some old habits die hard. I didn't mean anything by it, Jerry. Honestly, I didn't."

The jolly giraffe reached out his arm and rested it upon his friend's shoulder. "I know you didn't," he said, looking Leo firmly in the eye, "I know you didn't."

"If you two are finished," spat Mickey the monkey, "I would like to go inside now to see what all the fuss is about."

The jolly giraffe turned and smiled at Mickey the monkey. "Okay, Michael," he said softly, "I haven't seen you this excited since... well, ever."

The moaning monkey blew out his cheeks. "I have never been this excited," he said, shaking his head. "Now, can we please go inside?"

Without speaking, the three friends walked up to the polished metal door, smiling as it opened automatically.

"It smells even better inside," said Leo the lion, his mouth watering like a fountain. "Is it possible to order everything on the menu?"

The jolly giraffe laughed. "I suppose it is, Leo," he said, his eyes fixed on the giant screen that hung above the counter. "But I believe your eyes might be bigger than your belly. So, we will take a minute and look through the menu to see what you fancy the most."

"I know what I'm getting," said Mickey the monkey, licking his lips and bouncing on his tiptoes.

"You do?" said the jolly giraffe, casting his gaze between the flashing neon sign and his excited friend.

Leo the lion sighed. "It's just so overwhelming," he said, feeling his tummy rumble for a second time. "I mean, it's like an encyclopaedia of food."

"I know," said the jolly giraffe, "I have never seen such a plethora of food. I guess the best thing we can do is to narrow down our choices."

For the next few moments, the three friends stood in silence as the images on the silver screen swapped between pictures of tantalising food. There were hot dogs, sweet and sour dogs, and chilli dogs. There was jungle-fried chicken, barbecue ribs, and pulled pork with applesauce. There were sandwiches, toasted sandwiches, open sandwiches, sandwiches filled with every kind of meat possible. There were pizzas, large pizzas, medium pizzas; even the small pizzas were as big as a tractor's wheel. The duck was both roasted and honey-glazed. Tachos. Chilli tachos. Any meal plus a drink for fifteen ninety-nine.

"Fifteen ninety-nine, Jerry?" gasped the moaning monkey. "Did that just say fifteen ninety-nine?" The jolly giraffe stuttered. "I'm not sure, monkey," he said, keeping his gaze firmly fixed on the screen, "but you're not only paying for the food. You're also paying for the experience." The moaning monkey tutted and cast his eyes skyward. "I know it's lovely and all, Jerry," he said, turning his head in all directions, "but don't you think sixteen pounds is a bit extravagant for a burger and a plush red seat?"

"No," said the jolly giraffe, shaking his head, "look at the artwork on the walls and the crisp décor. You don't get that kind of detail down at Jungle King."

The moaning monkey nodded his head. "I suppose you're right, Jerry," he said, looking back up at the screen, "and let's be fair, the menu is amazing."

"The best I have ever seen," said Leo the lion, "how is one supposed to pick just one dish?"

"There's no need to rush, Leo," said the jolly giraffe, "we have all the time in the..."

"NEXT!" screeched a Leopard who was standing on a podium beside the counter. "NEXT!" "My goodness," said the jolly giraffe, rubbing his ear and opening and closing his mouth. "That is loud."

"What are you going to order, Jerry?" said the moaning monkey.

The jolly giraffe began to tremble. "I'm not sure," he said, feeling the sweat begin to break on his forehead. "There's just so much to choose from and so little time. I really did think we would have a little more time…"

"NEXT!" screeched the Leopard.

"Oh, monkey," shouted the jolly giraffe, his arms flailing wildly in the air, "what are we going to order?"

"Order anything," spat the moaning monkey, his heart beating loudly in his throat. "There's nothing on that menu I don't like."

Chapter Eight

The moaning monkey sat on the plush red seat with his arms folded tightly across his chest. "Is everything ok, monkey?" said the jolly giraffe, "you haven't spoken now for more than five minutes."

"Salad, Jerry," spat Mickey the monkey, "out of all the amazing food this place had to offer, you order salad?"

"I panicked, monkey," said the jolly giraffe, "that Leopard was giving me the evil eye."

Mickey the monkey tutted and threw his arms up into the air. "How do you know he was giving you the evil eye, Jerry? He's wearing sunglasses."

"Sunglasses" said the jolly giraffe looking over his right shoulder. "I don't think he was wearing sunglasses monkey."

"Well, he was" snapped Mickey the monkey, slamming the palms of his hands down onto the table. "If I say he was wearing sunglasses Jerry he was wearing sunglasses."

"Don't take it out on me, monkey," said the jolly giraffe after a long pause. "You know you always get this way when you're..."

"When I what?" interrupted monkey, the palms of his hands laying flat on the table. "I always get this way when I'm what?"

"Hangry," snapped the jolly giraffe, "you always get

cranky when you're tired and hungry."

Mickey the monkey gasped. "You take that back," he said, lifting his hand and placing it on his chest. "I am never hungry. The only thing I am right now is a little thirsty. Did you order drinks, Jerry?"

The jolly giraffe felt a knot of worry twist in his stomach. "Of course," he said, looking nervously over his shoulder, "I'm sure our friend Leopard over there understood our order perfectly well."

"That's good," said Leo the lion, "salad is fine with me. For a little moment there, I thought about ordering a burger. But I don't want to do that. I don't want to start eating meat." "Absolutely not," said the jolly giraffe, glancing sideways at Mickey the monkey, who looked like he had suddenly seen a ghost. "You're perfectly fine just the way you are, Leo."

Leo the lion smiled. "Thank you, Jerry," he said before yawning. "Now if you don't mind, I might nab some forty winks before the food arrives," he added, scratching his belly. "But don't panic if my eyes are open, I sometimes sleep that way especially when I'm overtired." "That's a great idea," said the jolly giraffe, "you grab a little nap, and we'll wake you when the food arrives."

For the second time in quick succession, Leo the lion yawned and scratched his belly. "Sounds good," he said, resisting his eyelids that now weighed the same as two bags of cement. "Sounds good."

In less time than it takes to count the fingers on one of the moaning monkey's hands, Leo the lion was sleeping soundly. For the next few minutes, they watched in silence as tray after tray of delicious food was dispatched from the kitchen and delivered to the surrounding tables by penguins dressed in penguin suits. "Love the dicky bow," sneered Mickey the monkey as another tray of piping hot food whizzed passed. "You must admire their skill," said the jolly giraffe, licking his lips at the stack of ribs that whizzed past. "What skill?" grumbled monkey. "Any fool can deliver food."

The jolly giraffe shook his head. "That's where you're wrong, monkey," he said, wagging his index finger, "it takes great skill to deliver food. Not to mention timing, endurance, memory function, and balance."

"Balance," scoffed mickey, eyeing up the massive plate of waffles that just got set down at the table adjacent to them. "You don't need much balance to move on roller skates." The jolly giraffe smiled. "Now come on, monkey, when did you ever deliver food on roller skates?"

The moaning monkey paused. "Never," he said, tearing a small piece of paper from the orange napkin, "but I once delivered pizza after parachuting from a plane."

The jolly giraffe giggled. "Oh, monkey," he said, "you're such a tease. You never delivered pizza after parachuting from a plane."

Mickey the monkey shrugged his shoulders. "You're right, Jerry," he said, brushing the pieces of spent paper from the table with his hand. "It wasn't the pizza I was delivering. It was glazed donuts."

The jolly giraffe purred like a cat. "Glazed donuts," he said, licking his lips, "do you think it's too late to order a tray of glazed donuts, Mickey?"

Mickey the monkey tilted his head and gazed over the shoulder of the sleeping beauty. "I don't know, Jerry," he said, shaking his head. "The line looks pretty long now. I'm guessing there's about an hour's wait."

The jolly giraffe sighed. "An hour," he said, drumming his fingers upon the table, "I don't think I can wait an hour for some donuts, mickey. No matter how well glazed they are." "Settle yourself, Jerry," said the Moaning monkey, "our food should be out shortly. We were just two behind those quarrelling squirrels, if you remember. And their food has just been delivered."

The jolly giraffe rubbed his hands together. "I'm so excited," he said, his face stretched into a smile. "I know it's only salad I ordered. But apparently, it's the nicest salad this side of the Amazon."

The moaning monkey nodded his head but remained silent. He watched as tray after tray of delicious cuisine whizzed past their table and was delivered to the hungry customers with a smile.

"That's it," snapped Mickey the monkey after watching a tray of honey-glazed ribs be devoured by a pack of hungry hyenas. "We've waited long enough, Jerry. I'm calling the manager." "The manager?" whispered the jolly giraffe, "do you think that's a good idea, monkey?" "Probably not," hissed Mickey the monkey, "but we have been sitting here for nearly three hours, and if we're not careful, we will soon be in the presence of very a hungry lion." The jolly giraffe swallowed hard. "I hear you, Mickey," he said, casting his eyes at the sleeping lion. "We need to have something on the table when Leo wakes up. Otherwise…"

"Shhhhhhhhh," whispered monkey, his index finger pressed against the jolly giraffe's lips. "Don't say it, Jerry. I'll just call the manager and see what the hold-up is with our food." The jolly giraffe nodded and watched as Mickey the monkey stopped one of the well-dressed penguins and asked politely if he could speak with the manager. "The manager," said Percy, his empty tray folded neatly under his arm. "I'll get him right away for you, sir. If you can just bear with me for two minutes."

Chapter Nine

Mickey the monkey doubted that the manager of Ravenous Rhinos would present himself in under two minutes. "There's no need to do that," said the jolly giraffe, watching his friend set the timer on his phone. "I'm sure the man's busy."

"Busy or not," snapped Mickey, "you shouldn't make promises that you can't keep." As the seconds ticked down, the jolly giraffe watched the smug smile on Mickey the monkey's face grow wider and wider. "Twenty seconds, Jerry," he said, rubbing his hands together with glee.

"Ten. Nine. Eight. Seven. Six. Five. Four. Three...."

"How can I be of assistance?" came a call from over the jolly giraffe's right shoulder. When the jolly giraffe turned, his gaze was met by the hulking frame of Ross the rhinoceros, the manager of Ravenous Rhinos. The jolly giraffe did not speak; instead, he lifted his hand and pointed towards his friend who sat squirming in his seat. "How can I be of assistance?" repeated the horned hulk, his voice booming through the booth. Mickey the monkey drummed his fingers on the table and whistled quietly to himself. "Go on, monkey," said the jolly giraffe, "tell the manager our complaint." Mickey the monkey shrugged his shoulders. "It's not really a complaint," he said, his eyes closed while the palms of his hands were held up for everyone to see, "it's more of an observation."

"An observation?" growled Ross, scribbling something down on his clipboard. "And what was it you observed?"

The moaning monkey laughed nervously. "You know," he said, shifting uneasily in his seat, "it's probably nothing. It's probably just a big misunderstanding."

Ross the rhinoceros nodded his head. "A misunderstanding," he growled, jotting down another note with his pencil. "Well, if that's all it is then," he said, turning, "I shall be on my way." The jolly giraffe looked at monkey, then turned and looked at the rhinoceros, then back to Mickey. "That's not all," he said, pushing up from the table. "We have a very serious complaint here. And I think you should hear it." Ross the rhinoceros

stopped dead in his tracks, turned, and ambled back towards the table. "Now sir," he said, licking the top of his pencil, "what seems to be the problem?"

The jolly giraffe coughed into his fist. "Well," he said, "we have been sitting here for nearly four hours...."

"Hold on," interrupted Ross, holding up his right hand as if he was stopping traffic. "You have been sitting here for four hours?"

"Yes," screeched the jolly giraffe. "We have been sitting here for four hours. Patiently, I might add," he added, waving his index finger. "We have been very patient up to this point. And still, no one has come over with our order."

"Who did you place your order with?"

"Salad," said the jolly giraffe.

Ross the manager shook his head. "No. No," he said, his grey face hard like stone. "Who did you place your order with? Not what you ordered."

"Oh, my bad," said the jolly giraffe, feeling his face fluster a little. "We placed our order with him."

Ross the rhinoceros turned to where the jolly giraffe was pointing, then turned back, then turned back again. "Now let me get this straight," he said, his hand placed firmly on his hip.

"You placed your order with Levi the Leopard."

"Yes," said the jolly giraffe sheepishly, "the leopard took our order."

Ross the rhinoceros smiled. Then he snorted. Then he snorted again, and then he burst out laughing. He laughed and he laughed. He laughed so loud that the rest of the restaurant stopped eating and turned to see what all the commotion was about. "I'm afraid," he said, wiping a tear from his eye, "that Levi, our Leopard friend over there, is deaf."

"What now?" said the jolly giraffe.

Ross the manager snorted once more and shook his head. "I'm afraid that our friend over there is a deaf leopard."

"A deaf leopard?" said the jolly giraffe, his face awash with concern. "What do you mean he's a deaf leopard?"

"I mean," said Ross the rhinoceros, leaning in towards the table, "he can't hear. He's deaf. He's a deaf leopard."

The jolly giraffe stuttered. "Buttttttt.... But I don't understand. If he's deaf, why is he taking orders?"

"Oh, Levi doesn't take orders," said the manager. "His job is to wait until one of the cashiers is free, and he shepherds people toward the counter."

"He doesn't shout 'next,' does he?"

Ross the manager nodded. "That's precisely what he shouts," he said.

Mickey the monkey jumped up onto the table. "Can we order now?" he said, standing in a Spider-Man pose.

"I'm afraid the kitchen is closed, sir," said Ross, shaking his head at the request. "But if you are willing to wait. Let me see," he paused and turned the face of his watch up to his. "Four hours," he said firmly. "If you can hang around for another four hours, breakfast is served at six."

"Six," said the jolly giraffe, his gaze cast sideways at the sleeping lion. "I don't think we can wait till six, monkey."

The moaning monkey swallowed hard. "Absolutely not," he said, looking anxiously at Leo.

"What do you think we should do now, Jerry?"

"I think we should move, monkey," said the jolly giraffe, sliding back his chair. "We should move as slowly and quietly as we possibly can."

"Good idea," whispered Mickey the monkey, so quiet that the jolly giraffe barely heard. Slowly and quietly, the two friends got up and tiptoed out of the restaurant. "If we hurry, monkey," said the jolly giraffe, "we can catch the twenty-four-hour shop before it closes." "Cool," whispered Mickey the monkey, glancing back over his right shoulder at the snoozing lion. "Very cool indeed, Jerry."

THE END

Printed in Great Britain
by Amazon